ISBN : 978-0-9977181-5-7
Visit www.monkeymantra.com

Before we begin about HOLI

What is Holi (Ho-lee)?

Holi is India's Festival of Colors and marks the end of winter and the start of spring.

Holi also celebrates love, friendship, and the triumph of good over evil.

When is Holi celebrated?

Holi is celebrated on the day after the last full moon of winter, usually in February or March.

How is Holi celebrated?

Holi is a fun and messy gathering where friends and family splash and spray colors on each other.

Flowers and Rangoli (*ran-go-lee*) decorate the streets and homes with lots of sweets made for the festival.

In some parts of India, a large bonfire called Holika Dahan (*ho-lee-ka   da-haan*) is lit the night before.

Holika was an evil demon princess who met her end in flames. The bonfire symbolizes burning all evil.

Why are colors used on Holi?

According to Indian mythology, Lord Krishna was dark, often described as blue in color.

Krishna liked Radha but was hesitant to tell her so.

He assumed that Radha would not like him because of his skin color.

Krishna's mother lightheartedly suggested that he apply color on Radha's face, so they look the same.

Krishna took his mother's advice earnestly and applied color on Radha.

And thus began their friendship, love, and the tradition of a colorful Holi!

LIFE

KRISHNA

LOVE

GOOD LUCK

Before we begin

Krishnanattam (krish -na - nat - tam)

Krishnanattam is a classical Indian dance and drama style that originated in the 16th century. Male dancers dressed in elaborate costumes and colorful masks, enact legends of Lord Krishna in eight plays. A combination of colors on the mask identifies the character in the play.

Green with bright red lips represents gods, divine characters, and the hero of the play.
Red portrays evil. Monks, sages, and female characters are yellow.
Black symbolizes forest dwellers, hunters, and demons.
A vibrant orange or saffron color is for divine characters.

Rangoli (ran - go - lee)

Rangoli is a traditional Indian art form where colorful patterns and shapes are drawn on the floor using powdered color.
The word "Rangoli" translates to "lines or layers of color" and is considered auspicious and drawn in front of homes and courtyards to welcome deities and bring good luck.

Pichkari
(pitch - kaa - ree)

Pichkari is a type of squirt gun used to spray color on Holi. The piston is pulled to pull in the colored water and pushed to spray the colored water out.

Burfi
(bur -fee)

Burfi is a traditional Indian sweet made from milk and is available in various flavors and colors. Shops that sell sweets and people who make them are called **Halwai** (Hal - wah -ee).

Holi COLORS!

Written and Illustrated by

Deven Jatkar

MONKEY MANTRA

Maya loved splashing and spraying colors and looked forward to Holi every year.
For Maya, Holi was a burst of colorful activities.
And every Holi she would...

Draw Rangoli with mom.

Weave Marigold garlands.

Decorate the house with dad.

Watch Holi Bonfire with grandfather.

Cook sweets with grandmother.

Help grandfather taste some sweets.

Clean Pichkaris.

Practice Pichkari Skills.

Gaze at the full moon

Buy Holi colors

with THE GANG !

Play Holi with family and friends.

And then, Maya would wait for a year.

Finally, it was the day before Holi.

Maya and her grandfather walked home from a Krishnanattam[1] show.

1.Krishnanattam (Krish-na-nat-tam): Classical Indian dance and drama syle that enacts the legends of Lord Krishna (Krish-naa).

It was Maya's first Krishnanattam show,
and back home, she told her grandmother all about it.

He had a green face!

And a red beard!

MEMORIES

Maya had plenty of activities planned for today.
She looked forward to meeting her friends later to buy Holi colors.
Suddenly, Maya heard her grandfather call.

Maya ran toward her grandfather but didn't notice her favorite kaleidoscope.

7

Maya fell, and everything around her went dark.

Maya woke up to her mother staring at her. But she was *blue!*
Maya jumped out of her bed.

As she ran past the mirror, Maya screamed! She was *red!*
And everything else was a mix of black, white, and grey!

Maya screamed so loudly that her family rushed in.
Her dad looked yellow, her brother green
and her grandparents violet!

Maya, what's wrong?

Maya's family didn't understand why she was upset.
And Maya was scared to talk to her different-looking family
in a different-looking world.

Maya's parents spent a long time trying to comfort her, but she wouldn't stop wailing.

Finally, Maya sobbed as her unfamiliar mom cuddled her.

Maya's brother laughed at her.
(He was as mean as ever.)

Maya's grandparents read her favorite book. They made the same funny faces and noises as they always did.

13

Brownie was as playful as ever.
Maya felt a bit better.

Be careful.

To cheer her up,
Maya's dad asked her to meet
her friends as she had planned.

Maya looked through the kaleidoscope.
The small, colorful beads looked black and white now.
But they still created her favorite wonderful dancing patterns.
Maya decided to take her favorite toy with her.

And Maya walked out to meet her friends.

Maya liked to wander into the florist's store and gaze at flowers.
Today was different - the variety of roses now looked the same.
But they still had the same lovely fragrance and sharp thorns!

At the Halwai[1], Maya was hesitant to try a sample.
Her favorite red and green burfi[2] looked simple and dull.
Reluctantly she took a bite. It tasted just as warm, gooey, and delicious!

1. Halwai (hal - wah -ee): Sweet shop.
2. Burfi (bur - fee): Traditional Indian sweet.

Maya walked past the store that sold Holi colors.
How could she play Holi if all the colors looked the same?

Maya's friends ran out of the Holi store to meet her.
"Why are you walking away from the colors store?" they asked, surprised.
Maya lamented about her color chaos to her puzzled friends.

What fun was Holi without the burst of colors she loved?
And then Maya noticed the Holi colors dazzling on her friend's hands. And Maya exclaimed
"Even if all the Holi colors look white, they will still glow on your colorful faces!"

Maya chose her friend's favorite Holi colors at the store.
And then Maya and her friends had a blast in the market, just as they did every year!

24

Maya walked home in the bright and hot afternoon sun.

The trees, the birds, the buildings, the cars...

Everything looked black, white, and grey.

But the people were all colorful.

Maya's town now looked like a gigantic kaleidoscope!

26

Maya came home and put her kaleidoscope and colors down.
When she heard her name called, she ran toward the voice.
She forgot about the kaleidoscope and colors in front of her.

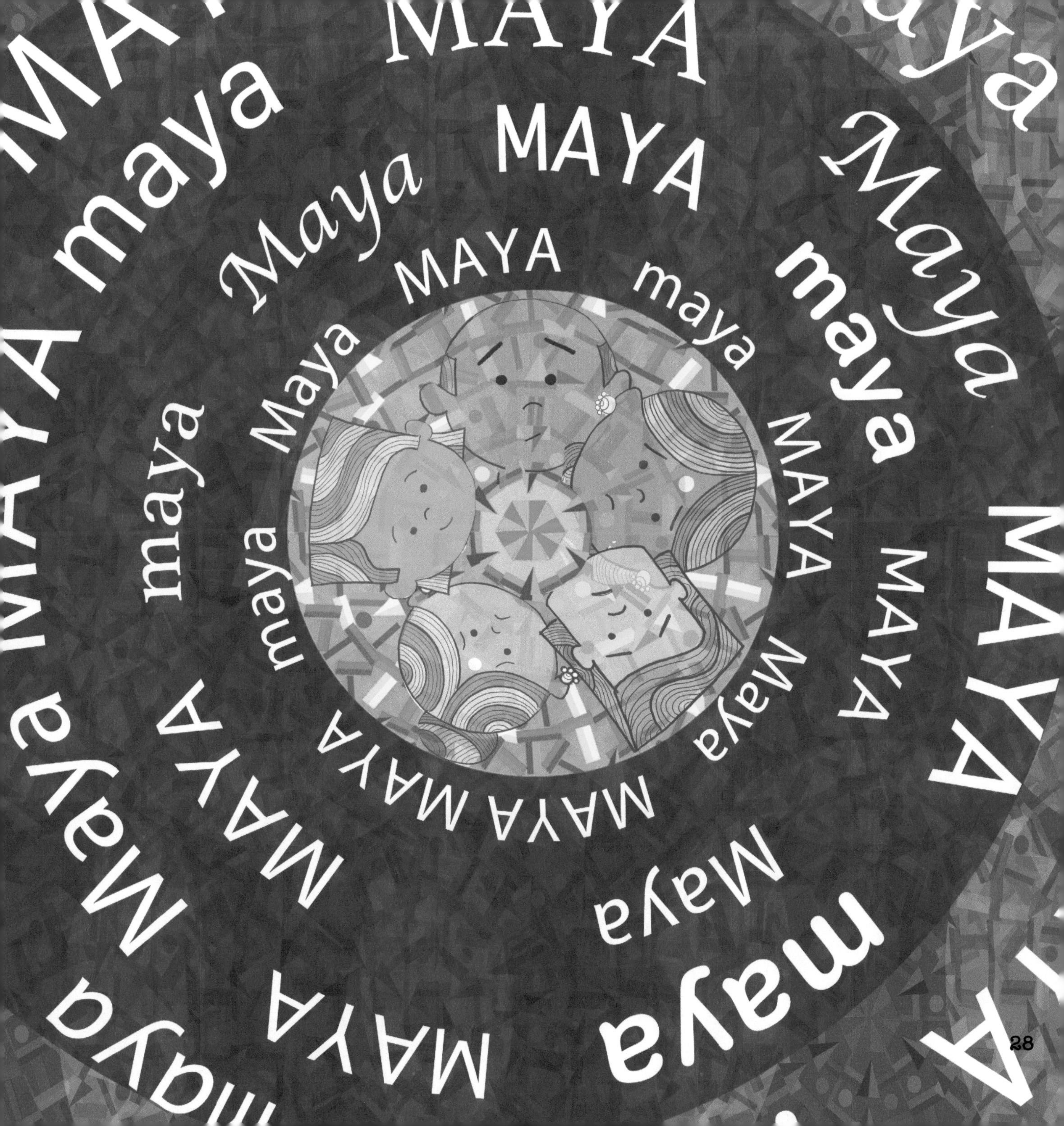

Startled, Maya woke up.
She'd been dreaming all this time!
"How are you feeling, Maya?" Her mom asked
Maya told them about her scary dream and grabbed her kaleidoscope.

The designs inside were just as beautiful as in her color chaos dream.

"Even if the beads changed color," Maya said,

" It did not stop them from creating beautiful patterns."

And then, Maya and her brother practiced their Pichkari[1] skills for tomorrow.

1.Pichkari (Pitch - kaa - ree): Squirt gun for spraying colored water.

Maya, her friends, and her family played Holi the next day.

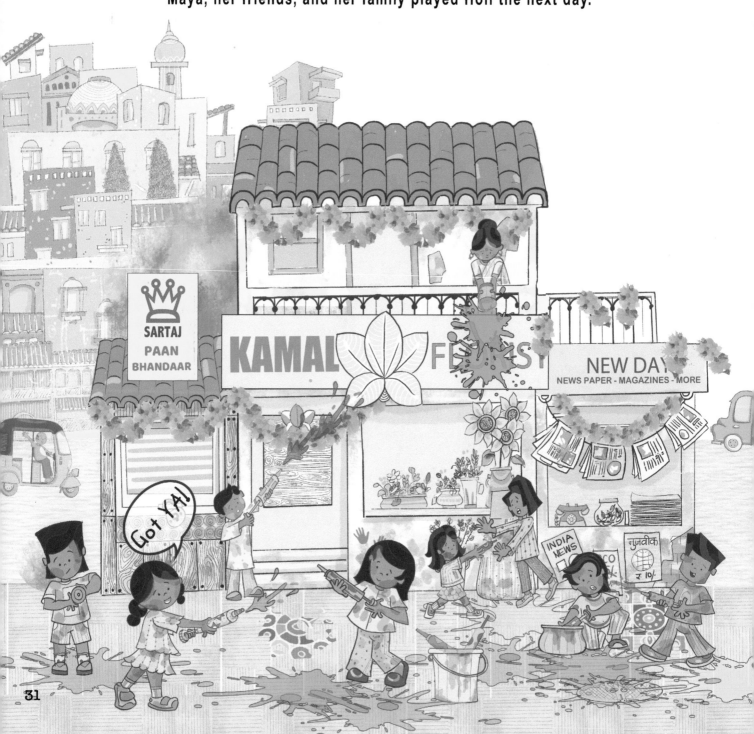

31

Love and friendship are forever,
Holi colors, she now knew, would eventually wash away!

I love all colors!

I love all colors!

I love all colors!

I love all colors!

~~I love all COLORS!~~

~~COLORS!~~

~~COLORS!~~

ISBN : 978-0-9977181-5-7

Visit www.monkeymantra.com

MONKEY MANTRA

CPSIA information can be obtained
at www.ICGtesting.com
Printed in the USA
LVHW072314130422
716130LV00002B/9